Witches Don't Do Backflips

There are more books about the Bailey School Kids!
Have you read these adventures?

Vampires Don't Wear Polka Dots
Santa Claus Doesn't Mop Floors
Leprechauns Don't Play Basketball
Werewolves Don't Go to Summer Camp
Ghosts Don't Eat Potato Chips
Frankenstein Doesn't Plant Petunias
Pirates Don't Wear Pink Sunglasses
Aliens Don't Wear Braces
Genies Don't Ride Bicycles

Witches Don't Do Backflips

by Debbie Dadey
and
Marcia Thornton Jones

illustrated by John Steven Gurney

A
LITTLE APPLE
PAPERBACK

SCHOLASTIC INC.

New York   Toronto   London   Auckland   Sydney

ISBN 0-590-48112-6

Text copyright © 1994 by Marcia Thornton Jones and Debra S. Dadey.
Illustrations copyright © 1994 by Scholastic Inc.
All rights reserved. Published by Scholastic Inc.
APPLE PAPERBACKS is a registered trademark of Scholastic Inc.

31 30 29 28 27   2/0

Printed in the U.S.A.   40

First Scholastic printing, September 1994

Book design by Laurie Williams

To Rebekah Dadey and Collin Baker —
may your lives be full of magic!

With thanks to Amanda and Kevin Gibson for
technical advice — DD and MTJ

Contents

Contents

1

Pink Tights and Tutus

"There's no way I'm going to wear funny-looking black tights," Eddie told Liza, Melody, and Howie. The kids were on their way to Brewbaker's Gym. Brewbaker's was a new gym and many third-graders from Bailey Elementary School had signed up for gymnastics classes there. First the four friends had stopped off at Eddie's aunt's house to feed her dog, Prince Diamond. Eddie promised to feed and to take care of her full-blooded Dalmatian while she was on vacation in Las Vegas.

When Eddie lifted the latch to slip out of the backyard, Diamond darted out. Eddie lunged after him, but all he caught was a mouth full of dried leaves as he fell on his face.

1

Melody giggled. "You look like you could use a few gymnastics lessons!"

Eddie spit out a twig and glared at her. "You can forget about any sissy lessons until we catch Diamond. Aunt Mathilda will cook us for dinner if anything happens to her new dog!"

Eddie and his friends chased after Prince Diamond, but the big spotted dog was too fast for them. He zigzagged around the front yard until the four friends were out of breath from chasing him.

"We'll be late for our first class if we don't catch him soon," Liza whined.

Howie shrugged. "I think he just wants some company. Why don't you let him come with us?"

Melody nodded. "Maybe he'll learn something besides scratching fleas."

"All right," Eddie agreed, "but it would be fine with me if we missed a silly tumbling class." As the four kids walked away from Aunt Mathilda's house, Prince Diamond trotted along beside them.

Melody laughed as she hurried along. "I think Eddie would look great in a pink tutu."

"That's it!" Eddie turned to walk away. "You won't catch me wearing any frilly ballerina stuff. I'm not going."

Howie grabbed his friend's arm. "This isn't ballet. It's gymnastics. And you're not going anywhere. If I have to do this, then so do you. Now, come on or we'll be late."

"Why does your mother want you to take lessons, anyway?" Eddie asked and continued walking with his friends.

Howie shrugged and watched a robin sitting on a fence post. "She said it'll help me be more graceful."

"Graceful!" Eddie yelled. "Boys don't need to be graceful!"

"My dad said football players take

dance and gym classes," Liza said. "It helps them to be more flexible."

"They probably wear pink tights and tutus," Melody giggled.

Eddie reached for Melody's pigtails. "I'll show you what I think of tutus."

"Quiet." Howie pointed to the gym at the end of Forest Lane. "There's somebody out front."

The four kids looked at the new building. It was two stories of solid black glass; even the door was black. In front was a porch of black marble with big black columns. Sweeping the porch was a short-haired figure dressed in black tights, black sneakers, and a black baseball cap.

"It's the teacher," Liza whispered. "Her name is Miss Brewbaker. I met her when Mom signed me up for the class."

"I've never seen so much black in my life. Hasn't she ever heard of colors?" Melody asked.

"It's depressing if you ask me," Howie said.

"Gymnastics lessons are depressing," Eddie complained.

"Don't be such a worrywart," Melody said. "I bet it'll be fun."

"Just like the black plague," Eddie mumbled. The woman on the porch stopped her sweeping, pulled the black baseball cap firmly down on her head, and waved at the kids.

Liza, Melody, and Howie waved back, but Eddie giggled. "Take a look at the size of her nose. If she sneezes, we'll end up somewhere over the rainbow. Look, she even has a wart on that huge honker."

"Eddie," Liza said softly. "That's not a wart. It's a mole. Besides, she can't help the size of her nose."

"Just like you can't help having red hair and freckles and being rude," Melody told Eddie.

Eddie held up his hands. "Don't get

your pigtails tied in a knot. I wasn't making fun of her. I was just stating facts."

"The fact is she's a nice lady who's going to show us how to do flips and cartwheels," Liza said.

"We'd better go inside and get this over with," Howie muttered.

"Don't worry," Liza told him. "It'll be good exercise."

Eddie shook his head. "Yeah, I wonder what kind of torture that 'nice lady' has in store for us."

2

Flying

Miss Brewbaker smiled and propped her broom against a shining black column as the kids walked up the yellow brick sidewalk.

"Somebody should have taught her to floss," Eddie snickered softly. "Then she wouldn't have lost that tooth."

Melody elbowed Eddie in the side and whispered, "She's not missing a tooth. That's just a big space in front. Lots of people have them."

"Like the space you have between your ears?" Eddie muttered.

Melody stuck her tongue out at him and then smiled at Miss Brewbaker. "We're here for gymnastics."

"Of course," Miss Brewbaker said in a deep voice. "Follow me." She turned and disappeared inside the black door. The four kids looked at each other. Howie shrugged and climbed the stairs.

"I hope she's a better teacher than she is a dresser," Eddie said.

"My mom says Miss Brewbaker is a top-notch gymnast from Europe." The four kids looked behind them at Carey, a girl from their class. Carey skipped up the steps, her blond hair bouncy and full of curls.

"What happened to your hair?" Howie asked.

"It looks like she fell in a bucket of hair curlers," Eddie joked.

Carey patted her curls. "I got a permanent." She smiled and turned around so everyone could see the back of her head.

"Miss Brewbaker may be a good gymnast," Melody said, ignoring Carey and pointing to the doorway, "but she's a terrible house cleaner. She could at least knock down these spiderwebs."

"We'll do it for her," Liza suggested, reaching for the broom.

"NO!" Miss Brewbaker shouted as she appeared in the doorway.

"We don't want to waste valuable tumbling time. Please, come in." Then she pointed a long fingernail at Prince Diamond. "But make sure that horrible, mangy mutt stays outside."

Diamond whined and lay down under a tall tree. Overhead, a squirrel skipped along a branch and chattered. When the squirrel hopped on to a telephone wire and scrambled around the building, Diamond dashed after him.

"That ought to keep Diamond busy during our class," Eddie said as the kids followed the gym teacher inside.

Miss Brewbaker led them past a steep staircase and down a dark hallway. Their footsteps echoed on the black-and-white tile floor.

"For a new building it's awfully dark," Liza said softly.

Miss Brewbaker peered down at her and smiled, showing the large gap between her teeth. "Sorry about that we haven't finished putting in all the lighting in the halls yet." Then she led them into a large room. It was completely empty, except for black mats covering the floor.

"Ick!" Liza called out. She pointed to a big, black spider crawling across the floor.

Miss Brewbaker smiled. "Do not be frightened of the spider. She is quite harmless."

"I hope this class is harmless," Howie blurted.

"We don't think we'll like gymnastics," Eddie told Miss Brewbaker.

Miss Brewbaker looked at Eddie and pulled her baseball cap firmly down on her head. Then she pushed a button on a tape recorder. The strong beat of a rock song made the windows rattle. Miss Brewbaker put her hands on her hips and yelled, "Watch what you can learn! You may even get to perform at the festival this month." Every year Bailey Elementary had a Halloween festival.

Miss Brewbaker clapped her hands and winked. Then she ran and did three cartwheels in a row without using her hands. Her body swirled through the air like a giant black cloud.

"Wow! That lady can move!" Howie whistled.

Carey nodded. "I told you she was good."

When Miss Brewbaker reached the end of the mat she did three backflips, jumping so high it was as if she hung in mid-air.

"Look at her soar!" Melody squealed.

Eddie stared at Miss Brewbaker and slowly nodded his head, "You're right, it DOES look like she's flying."

3

Rhyme Time

Miss Brewbaker did another backflip and landed right beside the five kids. Melody and Liza clapped their hands and Howie nodded. But Carey put her hands on her hips and shook her head. "I can't do that," she wailed. "It'll mess up my new hairdo!"

"You have such pretty golden locks," Miss Brewbaker purred. She reached out

and touched one stray curl. Then she winked and spoke deeply in a singsong voice:

> *"Straight or curly*
> *Black or gold*
> *You'll love tumbling*
> *When all is told!"*

Carey stood off to the side, watching the other kids try their luck at somersaults and cartwheels. She laughed every time Liza tried to do a cartwheel.

"Quit laughing at her," Melody warned. "You're not doing any better."

Carey shook her head so her curls swirled around her face. "I could, but I don't want to mess up my hair."

"If anything was going to mess that mop up, it would be the way you keep slinging it around," Melody told her. "You're just using your hair as an excuse."

"Am not!" Carey snapped.

"Then prove it," Eddie dared.

"Okay, I will!" Carey went to the end of the mat and took a deep breath. She took a tiny hop and skip before sending her feet sailing in a perfect cartwheel.

"Lovely!" Miss Brewbaker clapped from a corner of the room. "You are a very talented gymnast."

Carey smiled. "I'll bet that I can get even better with practice!" Then she cartwheeled across the room so fast, her legs looked like the spokes of a wheel.

"Wow," Liza sighed, "it's just like Miss Brewbaker said."

"That's right," Eddie said slowly. "Her rhyme came true."

Howie grinned. "If only she'd help Liza do a cartwheel, too."

Carey walked across the mat like the winner of a gold medal in the Olympics. "Liza always ends up sitting down hard on her rear."

"Be quiet," Melody snapped. "You'll hurt her feelings."

"But it's so funny," Carey giggled. She was right. Liza just couldn't get her legs straight up. Instead, they always swung sideways, throwing her off balance. By the end of the lesson, Liza was in tears.

"I'll never be able to do it," Liza sniffed.

Miss Brewbaker glided over the mats. She wiped a tear from Liza's cheek and patted her on the back. Then she spoke in her deep singsong voice:

"Replace that frown,
No time to cry!
Keep on practicing and
Soon you'll fly!"

Liza looked up at Miss Brewbaker. "Do you really think I can?"

"I know so!" Miss Brewbaker said firmly. "Now try once more."

Liza looked at her friends and sniffed

before running down toward the mat.

Howie clapped and Melody did a little cheer as Liza finished a perfect cartwheel. "Yeah! You did just as well as Carey!"

Liza grinned and clapped her hands. "It's so easy all of a sudden."

Eddie didn't say a word. The other four kids said good-bye to Miss Brewbaker and then all five gymnasts walked onto the porch. The black glass door slammed shut behind them.

"Isn't he adorable?" Liza pointed to a fat cat perched on the porch. The cat stopped licking his paws to blink his huge amber eyes at the kids.

Eddie took one look at the cat and said, "My grandmother says black cats are bad luck."

"I think he's cute," Liza said and petted the cat until he closed his eyes and purred.

"That's Merlin, my cat," Miss Brewbaker told them as she stepped on to the porch with her broom.

"Merlin, what a ridiculous name for a cat," Eddie said after they were on the sidewalk, away from Miss Brewbaker.

"Merlin was the wizard in the King Arthur stories," Howie said. "My dad read them to me. Merlin was pretty neat."

"I like that name," Liza said. "It's magical."

Eddie looked back at the tall black building, the black cat, and the high flying gymnastics teacher sweeping the porch. "Magical is just the right word," he said softly.

4

Witch's Broom

Eddie slurped the last of his chocolate milk and looked at his friends. "Don't you think Miss Brewbaker is odd? Normal people don't talk in rhymes." Eddie, Liza, Melody, and Howie sat at the kitchen table at Melody's house, having a snack.

"I think she's neat," Liza said, munching on a chocolate chip cookie.

"You just like her because she showed you how to do a cartwheel," Melody said.

"That *was* strange," Howie said. "Right after Miss Brewbaker said that rhyme, Liza did a perfect cartwheel."

"The same thing happened with Carey," Eddie pointed out.

Liza slowly sipped her milk. "That's

because Miss Brewbaker is a good teacher."

Eddie threw his napkin into the trash can. "If you ask me, there's something spooky going on at that gym."

"I wasn't going to say anything, but I noticed something, too," Howie said. "When we went inside, Miss Brewbaker left her broom on the porch."

"So?" Melody said. "My mom does that all the time."

"But when we went outside, the broom wasn't there. Miss Brewbaker carried it with her when she came outside." Howie wiped his mouth with a paper napkin and looked at his friends.

"A broom can't move itself," Melody said.

"Not unless it's a magical broom," Eddie told them.

Melody giggled. "I think Eddie's in la-la land."

Eddie ignored Melody. "Think about it.

It all adds up: a moving broom, strange rhymes that come true, and flips that look like flying."

"It adds up to what?" Liza asked.

Eddie slapped the table. "Don't you guys get it? Miss Brewbaker's a witch."

Liza and Melody broke into a fit of giggles. "That cold milk froze Eddie's brain," Melody snickered.

"Miss Brewbaker is not a witch," Liza blurted.

Melody nodded. "Liza's right. Witches don't teach gymnastics."

"And they definitely don't do backflips," Liza added. "Haven't you ever read any fairy tales? Witches fly through the air on brooms."

"Exactly," Eddie interrupted. "Just like Miss Brewbaker's broom. If she's a witch, it would explain how the broom moved."

"You have to admit," Howie told the girls, "it was pretty creepy the way Carey and Liza were able to do cartwheels after

Miss Brewbaker chanted those rhymes."

Melody stood up from the table. "I can't believe you could be so silly. You're just saying this because she has a big nose and a wart."

"A mole," Liza reminded her.

"Whatever," Melody said. "People can't help the way they look."

"Melody's right. You're being mean. I think you're just trying to get out of taking gymnastics. Miss Brewbaker's great and I'm not afraid of her. As a matter of fact, I'm going back there right now," Liza said.

"Why?" Howie asked. "The next class isn't until tomorrow."

Liza shrugged. "I forgot my gym bag and it has my house key in it."

Melody looked out the window. It was already starting to get dark. "Why don't you stay here? You can call your mom at work."

"No." Liza shook her head. "I've already

lost one house key. Mom was mad because we had to change all the locks.
You're not afraid of Miss Brewbaker, are
you?"

Melody shook her head. "I'm not
afraid."

Eddie shook his head and muttered,
"I'm not afraid, but I'm not going back
there."

"Yes, you are," Melody said and

grabbed Eddie by the arm. "Be right back," Melody yelled to her mom.

The four kids walked out of Melody's house and back toward Brewbaker's Gym with Prince Diamond trotting behind them. Several dogs barked at them as they strode through the neighborhood.

The building was totally dark as the kids walked up the yellow brick sidewalk. A flock of crows flew overhead. "This

place is creepy in the evening," Howie gulped.

"It doesn't look like anyone's here," Melody said.

"Liza, why'd you have to leave your bag?" Eddie complained.

"Yeah," Howie said, "I'd rather be home scrubbing trash cans than going inside here."

"It'll just take a second," Liza said as she walked up the shiny black steps. But before she could knock on the door, a small black creature slid across the porch and twisted itself around her legs.

"Aaahh!" Liza screamed. "It's got me!"

5

Frog Legs and Spider Stew

Liza jumped and knocked into Miss Brewbaker's broom, sending it crashing to the floor of the porch. The loud noise sent Diamond into a barking fit and the black animal at Liza's feet hissed. As soon as the dog noticed the cat, he flew up on the porch. Merlin arched his back, hissed, and quickly swatted the dog's wet nose before springing off the porch. Prince Diamond lunged after him and both animals raced around the building.

"It was just Miss Brewbaker's black cat," Melody said with relief. "There's no reason to be scared."

"I wouldn't be so sure," Eddie said. "A black cat is bad luck, especially when it's a witch's cat."

"You've got a hairball stuck in your

brain," Liza said. "I'm not afraid of a black cat. I was just startled, that's all."

Melody slapped Eddie on the back. "Your imagination is getting the best of you. There are no such things as witches or ghosts or goblins. And I'll prove it to you."

"How?" Howie asked.

"Easy. Liza's forgot her gym bag, right?"

Liza, Eddie, and Howie nodded.

"It's obvious that no one is here, so all we have to do is walk in and get Liza's bag. While we're at it, we'll take a quick look around. I'm willing to bet all my Halloween candy that we won't find anything but smelly old gym socks."

"We can't just walk in there," Liza told Melody. "That's snooping."

"We have to get your key, don't we?" Melody asked as she slowly pulled on the door. "Oh, no, it's locked," she said. "We'll have to go around back."

"What if someone sees us?" Howie warned. "They might call the police."

Melody shrugged. "We'll just tell the truth. We're looking for Liza's gym bag."

Melody stepped over Miss Brewbaker's broom and hopped down the shiny steps, leading her friends to the back of the gym. Long shadows covered the lawn and a chilly October breeze moaned through the tree branches. Somewhere in the distance they heard Prince Diamond howling. Melody tried the back door. Slowly, it opened. Inside, the building was pitch-black.

"Follow me," Melody whispered and went inside. "I think the gym is this way." The four kids walked down the wide empty hallway.

"I smell food," Howie said.

"There's supposed to be a health food snack bar here," Liza said.

"What if Miss Brewbaker is cooking frog legs and spider stew for a snack?"

Eddie said sarcastically as they waited for Melody to open a door.

"Hope you're hungry," Liza giggled.

The door slowly swung open, letting a sliver of light escape into the hall. "Oh, my gosh," Melody said, stepping back.

Her three friends pushed around her, gasping at what they saw.

"This proves it," Howie whispered.

6

Hansel and Gretel

The four kids stood in the middle of a small kitchen, staring at the biggest gingerbread house they'd ever seen. Its roof was covered with bright gumdrops and the sides were smothered with peppermint icing. Strawberry licorice outlined windows of lemon drops and the sidewalk was made out of jelly beans.

"That's a fabulous gingerbread house," Liza whispered. "It covers the whole table. I bet it took Miss Brewbaker days to make it."

Eddie nodded and reached out to pluck a gumdrop from the roof.

"Don't touch that!" Howie hissed.

"Why not?" Eddie asked. His hand was frozen over the colorful roof. "No one will miss one measly gumdrop."

"That's exactly what Hansel and Gretel thought," Howie told him. "And they almost ended up as witch pudding."

Liza shook her head. "Miss Brewbaker is not a witch but you shouldn't mess up her house. That took a lot of work to build."

"Come on," Melody said, "let's get your bag. The gym must be behind the other door." Melody turned to go out of the kitchen but then she stopped suddenly. "Wasn't Miss Brewbaker's broom on the porch?" she asked.

Liza nodded. "I knocked it over. We'll have to set it back up before we leave."

"We won't have to," Melody said with a tremble in her voice. "Because it's already been picked up and put away."

"What are you talking about?" Howie asked.

Melody pointed to the hall. There,

propped beside the door, was Miss Brewbaker's broom.

"How did it get there?" Liza asked.

"It flew," Eddie said seriously.

"Brooms don't fly on their own," Liza told him.

"You're right," Eddie whispered. "They usually come with a witch." Before his friends had a chance to say anything, a shrill cackling came from deep within the dark building.

"What's that?" Liza whimpered.

"I think Eddie's witch just flew in!" Melody said. "Let's get out of here."

"But I can't leave without my key," Liza cried.

"Come on!" Eddie called over his shoulder as he raced down the dark hall and out the back door.

"You'll stay with me, won't you?" Liza asked Melody.

Just then another haunting laugh sent goose bumps racing down their backs.

Melody's eyes got big and she slid around the broom, keeping her back to the wall. When another high-pitched screech echoed throughout the building, Eddie pushed Melody all the way out the back door.

Liza heard the back door shut, then she slowly headed for the only other door in the hallway.

7

Bubbling Brew

The building was deathly still as Liza crept down the long, dark hallway. "There's no such thing as witches. There's no such thing as witches," Liza whispered to herself. She didn't really believe Miss Brewbaker was a witch, but a moving broom and dark hallways were enough to scare her.

Finally, she reached the door and held her breath while she opened it. It was the gym, filled with black gym mats.

Outside, the brisk autumn wind rattled the tall tree's branches, making them scrape against the black window. Liza spied her gym bag nestled in the corner, and tiptoed across the soft mats. Just as she reached out to grab the handle, the room was flooded with light.

"Why, hello my little pretty," Miss Brewbaker said softly.

Liza jumped around and stared at Miss Brewbaker standing in the doorway, her arms loaded down with groceries. "I . . . I left my bag," Liza stammered. "My house key is inside."

Miss Brewbaker nodded. "I'm surprised you were able to get in. I thought I locked the door."

Liza looked down at the smudge on her sneaker. "We figured you already went home, so we tried the back door," she explained. "It wasn't locked. We saw your gingerbread house, too."

"I see." Miss Brewbaker smiled. "It will be a lovely donation for the Fall Festival, don't you agree?"

"The festival?" Liza whispered. "You made that beautiful house for the festival?"

"Of course," Miss Brewbaker told her. "What else would it be for?"

Liza started to tell her that witches used gingerbread houses to lure and trick kids, but instead she snapped her mouth shut. She didn't want to hurt Miss Brewbaker's feelings.

"Get your key and come with me," Miss Brewbaker told her. "You may help me with these groceries. I bought a few treats for my students."

Liza carried a bag of groceries into the small kitchen and watched while Miss Brewbaker took out a big black pot from a cabinet. "I thought I would have a warm drink before going home," she told Liza.

"Hot chocolate is my favorite," Liza said.

"This is not exactly hot chocolate," Miss Brewbaker said. "It is an ancient recipe passed down by my family. A secret recipe." Miss Brewbaker opened another cabinet and pulled out the oldest book Liza had ever seen. The cover was made from bumpy black leather and the pages were yellowed with age.

When Miss Brewbaker gently opened the book, dust floated like a cloud above the pages. She used a pointy black fingernail to follow the list of ingredients. Then she gathered six bottles from a shelf. They were filled with strange yellow and purple spices. Miss Brewbaker carefully sprinkled a pinch from each jar into the kettle, added some water, and stirred the mixture with a big wooden spoon.

When the mixture bubbled loudly, Miss Brewbaker took out two tall black mugs with pictures of cats on them and poured the brew into the mugs. To Liza, the mixture looked like thick pea soup.

"Would you like to join me?" Miss Brewbaker asked, holding the mug out so Liza could smell the spicy aroma.

Liza stared at the bubbling brew and

shook her head. "N . . . no thank you. I have to go home. Thanks for letting me get my gym bag, and it was nice of you to make that gingerbread house for the Fall Festival."

Miss Brewbaker shrugged. "It is only something I whipped up. Besides, Halloween is my favorite holiday."

Liza picked up her gym bag and took one last look at the beautiful gingerbread house before walking down the hall. "Good-bye, Miss Brewbaker," Liza yelled as she pulled open the back door.

When the door opened, Merlin darted in with Prince Diamond close behind.

"Diamond, get out of here!" Liza cried, racing after the big spotted dog. Both animals ran straight into the kitchen where Merlin jumped on the counter behind Miss Brewbaker. Diamond skidded to a stop and cocked his head. Before Liza could reach him, Diamond jumped up and licked Miss Brewbaker right across the nose. Miss Brewbaker wiped her face and pointed a skinny finger at Diamond before saying in a singsong voice:

> *"Leave us be,*
> *We don't like dogs.*
> *Especially spotted ones*
> *Like warty frogs!"*

Then Miss Brewbaker sneezed so hard, Prince Diamond dropped back down to the floor. His toenails clicked on the tile as he smelled around the kitchen. Prince Diamond whined once and then put his front paws on the table.

"Get that creature before he eats the gingerbread house!" Miss Brewbaker screamed. Then she sniffed, pointed at

Prince Diamond, and said in her singsong voice:

> "Hop away, hop away,
> You big bag of fleas.
> Get out of my kitchen
> And stay away. Please!"

"He doesn't mean any harm," Liza explained as she grabbed Prince Diamond's collar. "I'm sorry. I'll make sure he never gets in here again." Then Liza dragged Prince Diamond out the back door.

Liza kept her hand hooked in Prince Diamond's collar as she headed away from the gym. She was halfway down Forest Lane when Howie, Eddie, and Melody jumped out from behind a bush.

"We were just coming back for you," Melody explained. "We didn't mean to leave you there all by yourself."

Liza glared at her friends. "You did too. You're a big bunch of chickens!"

"We are not!" Eddie snapped.

"Then why did you run?"

Howie shrugged. "You could have come too."

Liza held up her bag. "I had to get my key and you know it. You should have helped me."

"At least we sent Prince Diamond in after you," Eddie defended himself.

"You did not," Liza told him. "He was chasing Merlin and he really made Miss Brewbaker mad."

Melody nodded. "I guess we panicked. We're sorry, aren't we?" Melody looked at Howie and Eddie, but they weren't listening anymore. They were too busy staring at Prince Diamond.

"Something is wrong," Howie said softly. "Something is very wrong!"

8

Frog City USA

Prince Diamond was whining and turning around in circles. Then he sniffed and took three steps back toward Brewbaker's Gym.

"Get back here," Eddie said sternly. Prince Diamond looked at Eddie and whined. Then, before anyone could stop him, the huge dog dashed down the street and disappeared into the shadows of the night.

"Diamond!" they all screamed at once. "Come back!"

But the night was quiet except for the wind blowing scattered leaves. "I have to get him, or Aunt Mathilda will have a fit."

"But it's already dark," Melody said. "We have to get home."

"Melody's right," Liza agreed. "We'll never find him now. We'll help you look for him first thing in the morning."

Howie nodded. "Diamond will probably go home on his own as soon as he gets hungry."

Eddie looked nervously down the street, hoping to catch a glimpse of Diamond. "Are you sure he'll be all right?"

"Positive," Howie said.

The next morning was Saturday. Liza,

Howie, Melody, and Eddie were up early, searching the neighborhood for Prince Diamond. They were worried about Aunt Mathilda's dog. The more they yelled for him, the more concerned they became.

"Diamond has never stayed away so long," Eddie told his friends. "He likes being a nuisance too much."

"Sort of like you," Melody kidded.

"This is no time for jokes," Eddie said. For once, he was totally serious. "Diamond is a good dog," he said. "I hope nothing's happened to him."

Liza patted Eddie on the back. "Don't worry. We'll find him."

"Maybe he's chasing Merlin again," Melody suggested.

Liza shook her head. "He'd better not. Miss Brewbaker would have a fit."

Howie rubbed his chin. "Liza, did Miss Brewbaker see Diamond last night after gym?"

"See him?" Liza said. "Why, Diamond practically kissed her on the lips."

"Oh, no!" Howie said. "It's worse than I thought."

"It's all right," Melody said. "No one ever died from kissing a dog. Kissing Eddie, maybe, but not a dog."

Howie ignored Melody and grabbed Liza's shoulders. "This is important, Liza. Did Miss Brewbaker say a rhyme about Diamond?"

"How did you know?" Liza asked. "She said two of them about frogs and dogs."

Eddie slapped his forehead. "Miss Brewbaker's done something to Diamond. My Aunt Mathilda is never going to believe this."

"Don't be silly," Liza told them. "Miss Brewbaker is *not* a witch and she didn't do anything to Diamond. That silly dog is probably sleeping in your Aunt Mathilda's backyard."

"I'll go check," Eddie said hopefully.

While Eddie jogged down the street, his three friends continued looking in nearby yards. They hadn't looked long when a scream sent them racing after Eddie.

Eddie stood in the middle of Aunt Mathilda's backyard. He pointed to the bottom of a weeping willow tree and screamed again as Howie, Melody, and Liza skidded to a stop in the grass.

"What's wrong?" Melody gasped.

Eddie turned to look at his friends. His face was as gray as the clouds in the sky. "We have to stop that tumbling mad woman!"

"What are you talking about?" Liza asked.

"I'm talking about what she did to Diamond!"

Howie, Melody, and Liza glanced around the yard. "I don't see anything," Howie said.

"Look closer," Eddie told them, pointing to a little green frog with big black spots.

Melody's eyes got big and Howie sucked in his breath.

"You don't really think that's Prince Diamond," Liza said.

Eddie crossed his arms and nodded like he'd just won a presidential debate. "I told you that Miss Brewbaker spelled trouble."

Melody kneeled down to pet the frog's bumpy skin. "You can't prove this is Diamond. For all we know, it's just a freckled frog."

"What if it is Diamond?" Howie asked. "We have to find out for sure."

"How?" Melody asked. "If she is a witch, she might turn us all into frogs!"

"There's only one thing to do," Howie said seriously. "We have to find out how to stop her. And I know where to find all the information we need."

Without another word, the four kids marched toward the Bailey City library with a little frog hopping close behind.

9

Operation Research

Dark storm clouds rolled over Bailey City and a cold wind sent leaves whirling. Rain splattered the windows of the library as Liza, Eddie, and Melody waited for Howie to find what he needed. He searched up and down several shelves until he spotted a fat green book. He carried it to the checkout desk and waited. Mr. Cooper was too busy talking to another librarian to notice them.

"It's got me in a dither," Mr. Cooper sighed. "I'm just lost without my little Snookems. The house is like a graveyard without her padding around the house after me, and I just can't sleep unless I hear Snookems's cute little bark."

The other librarian nodded. "Old Mrs. Farley says the same thing about her poodle. I can't imagine where those two dogs have wandered off to, but I'm sure both of them will turn up soon."

"Where could they be?" Mr. Cooper said with a hopeless sigh. "I've looked everywhere, but all I can find are nasty frogs."

Eddie gasped, and Howie nearly choked. "Did you say frogs?" Melody asked.

Mr. Cooper nodded at the children standing by the checkout desk. "I've never seen so many frogs before in my life. I guess that rainy spell we had last winter had something to do with it."

"It's a spell, all right," Eddie muttered.

"What did you say?" Mr. Cooper asked.

Howie shoved the big book he was holding at Mr. Cooper before Eddie could say anything else. As soon as Mr. Cooper saw the book, he shook his head. "You're always checking out this book. Maybe you should try reading something else,

like a good mystery. I'd be happy to show you some."

Howie smiled politely and shrugged. "It's a fat book. It takes a long time to read."

"Hummph," Mr. Cooper mumbled as he checked out the book and returned Howie's library card.

"Thank you," Howie said, grabbing the book and heading toward a table with his friends. "I hope you find your little dog!"

The four friends sat in a corner of the library. All around them, kids were reading fun holiday stories, but Liza, Howie, Melody, and Eddie didn't notice. They stared at Howie as he opened the big book to the index.

"What are you looking for?" Melody whispered.

"Proof," Howie answered. "I think Eddie's right about Miss Brewbaker being a witch, and I plan to figure out what we can do to get Diamond back."

Liza put her hands on her hips. "Miss Brewbaker didn't do anything to Diamond. He's probaby off chasing squirrels somewhere."

"Then explain the spotted frog being right where Prince Diamond likes to stretch out," Eddie dared her.

"Easy," she said. "It's just like Mr. Cooper said. The rainy weather brought tons of frogs to Bailey City."

"But what about Snookems and the poodle?" Howie asked.

Melody nodded. "I bet Miss Brewbaker zapped them into tiny little frogs."

Liza giggled. "Miss Brewbaker wouldn't do that. She's too nice."

Howie slowly shook his head. "I wish you were right, Liza. But I'm afraid Miss Brewbaker can't stand dogs. Remember she called Diamond a mangy mutt?"

"So?" Liza said. "I don't like hamsters, but that's not a crime!"

"It *is* a crime if you change dogs into frogs!" Eddie yelled.

"Shhh!" Mr. Cooper warned. "You children will have to hop along if you can't be quiet!"

"I wish he hadn't said hop!" Melody muttered.

Howie sighed. "I think those rhymes that Miss Brewbaker keeps saying are really witch spells."

Liza rolled her eyes. "That's not true! Miss Brewbaker is nice. After all, she showed me how to do a cartwheel."

Melody shrugged. "Cartwheels today and flying on broomsticks tomorrow."

Howie tapped the fat book in front of him. "I have a plan." The four kids huddled together as Howie shared what was in the book. "There are two ways to stop a witch's spell," he began.

"You're as batty as a witch's attic,"

Melody said as soon as Howie was finished.

Eddie stood up from the library table. "We have no choice. We have to help Prince Diamond . . . before it's too late."

10

Witch's Cookbook

The cold, drizzling rain continued as the four friends hurried to Brewbaker's Gym. A cool wind rattled the brightly colored leaves of the trees overhead.

Liza shook her head when they stopped in front of the black building. "I still don't think Miss Brewbaker is a witch. But I did notice something strange when I was in the kitchen."

"You mean besides the fact that she had a gingerbread house big enough to feed half of Bailey City?" Eddie asked.

Liza nodded. "Miss Brewbaker has a very unusual cookbook. She used it to make her brew. It's very old and too fancy to be an ordinary cookbook."

"Maybe it's a witch's cookbook!" Melody said.

"And it has recipes for spells!" Eddie agreed.

"Great!" Howie slapped his hands together. "Now that we know where the spell book is, I know just what to do. We'll keep Miss Brewbaker busy with gymnastics while one of us sneaks into the kitchen."

"Just be careful," Melody warned.

"Be careful about what?" Carey asked from behind them, causing all four kids to jump.

"We were talking about how dangerous gymnastics can be," Melody fibbed.

Carey flung her curls around her head and opened Miss Brewbaker's gate. "I'm so good, I don't have to worry about it. You're the ones who should be careful."

"I'd like to carefully rearrange your face," Eddie muttered before Howie pulled him onto the yellow brick sidewalk.

"Come on," Howie said. "We've got to help Diamond."

The black building's shiny windows stared down like evil eyes as the five children climbed the steps and pushed open the door. "Are you sure we should do this?" Melody asked.

Howie opened his mouth to answer, but he didn't have a chance. Just then Miss Brewbaker appeared with a big smile. She wore the same black baseball cap pulled down over her short hair, and she held a huge basket filled with shiny red apples. "Good morning, children. How about a snack before we get started?"

"Thanks," Eddie said and reached out to take the biggest apple.

Howie grabbed Eddie's arm, yanking it back. "We'd better not. We wouldn't want to get sick when we're turning flips."

Miss Brewbaker shrugged and went over to the mats. Liza and Carey ran over and started showing Miss Brewbaker their cartwheels.

Eddie frowned at Howie. "What's the big idea?" Eddie complained. "I was hungry."

"Did you just crawl out from under a rock?" Melody whispered. "Haven't you ever heard of *Snow White and the Seven Dwarfs*?"

"Yeah, and you're being just like that dwarf Dopey," Eddie giggled.

"You're the dope," Melody said under her breath. "The witch in that story puts Snow White to sleep by giving her a poison apple."

"Don't worry about me." Eddie smiled.

"I'm too tough for poison." He walked over to Miss Brewbaker and picked up the basket of apples.

"I'd be happy to take these to the snack bar for you," Eddie said sweetly. Eddie carried the basket past the kids. He licked his lips as he headed down the hall.

"You don't think Eddie would be stupid enough to eat one of those, do you?" Melody asked Howie softly.

Howie shook his head. "If he does, it will be the last thing he chomps down on. He'll be dreaming until a princess kisses him. And that would be forever!"

11

The End of Rhyme

"Come on over, children. I want to show you a new flip," Miss Brewbaker called to the class. "We have an exhibition tomorrow and this flip will impress your parents. It will be great practice for those of you chosen to perform at the Fall Festival."

The four kids concentrated on the flip Miss Brewbaker was showing them. She flung her legs up and did five flips in a row to the end of the mats and then did five more flips back to the kids.

"That's a round-off," Carey informed them. "I'm sure I can do it."

Miss Brewbaker smiled. "I'm sure everyone will be able to do it by the end of the lesson."

Howie shrugged his shoulders and

71

tried. He ended up in a lump on the floor. "This is dangerous," Howie complained. "I could have broken my neck!"

"You're right," Miss Brewbaker said. "Gymnastics can be very dangerous."

"Especially when your teacher is a witch," Melody mumbled to Liza. Liza shook her head and rolled her eyes.

Miss Brewbaker helped Howie up. "It is important to never try dangerous flips without a mat and an instructor. That is why I am here." Then Miss Brewbaker patted Howie on the head and chanted:

> *"Through the air*
> *You will fly,*
> *Never afraid*
> *Of soaring . . . "*

"High!" Howie hollered.

"Oh," Miss Brewbaker said, in surprise, "so you like to rhyme, do you?"

Howie nodded. "I've taken it up recently. So have my friends."

Melody, Liza, and Carey looked at each other. "We have?" Liza asked.

"How about this one?" Miss Brewbaker pulled her black baseball cap down firmly on her head and chanted:

> *"Up and down*
> *My broom will go*
> *With all the children*
> *Lined up in a . . . "*

"Row!" Howie shouted.

Miss Brewbaker stomped her foot, adjusted her hat, and did three backflips. Her body swirled through the air like a black fog.

"What are you doing?" Melody asked. "You're making her mad."

"The library book said that finishing a rhyme takes away the spell's power," Howie reminded her.

Miss Brewbaker did three backflips and turned up the visor of her cap. "How about this one," she said.

> *"Four little kiddies*
> *Too cute to stop*
> *Now is the time*
> *For you to . . . "*

"Hop!" Liza shouted and clapped her hands.

Miss Brewbaker looked at her and

jumped up and down. Then she bounced around the room faster and faster.

"I think Miss Brewbaker has flipped out," Carey said.

Melody ignored Carey and looked at Liza. "If you didn't believe she was a witch, why were you so quick at finishing that rhyme?"

Liza shrugged. "I said that just in case. I don't want to be a frog."

"Here we go again," Howie interrupted as Miss Brewbaker headed toward the

kids. "I hope you girls are good with rhymes."

Miss Brewbaker stopped her flipping and panted:

> *"Topsy-turvy,*
> *End over end*
> *You and I*
> *Were meant . . . "*

Howie, Melody, Liza, and Carey looked at each other.

"What's a word that rhymes with end?" Howie shouted.

Carey, Liza, and Melody shrugged their shoulders. Then suddenly Liza smiled and yelled, "Were meant to be friends!"

Miss Brewbaker pulled off her cap but instead of flipping, she smiled at Liza.

Liza smiled back at her and said:

*"We have won
This game of rhyme
As friends we'll have
A much better time!"*

Miss Brewbaker put her cap back on and started laughing. She pointed her finger at Liza and said:

*"I give up
You have me beat
But I like you kid,
I think you're neat!"*

"Do you really mean it?" Liza giggled.

Miss Brewbaker nodded. "Of course, I do. You are a wonderful tumbler and have a great ear for rhyme. I'd be proud to have you as my friend."

"What about Prince Diamond?" Howie asked.

Miss Brewbaker looked confused. "Who is Prince Diamond?"

Melody stepped forward. "Diamond is the big spotted dog that you turned into a frog!"

Miss Brewbaker's smile faded and she pulled her cap off. "Dogs don't interest me, especially ones that chase Merlin. Now, you must run along. Don't be late for tomorrow's exhibition."

The four kids grabbed their bags and ran out of the building. They didn't stop until they were at the end of the yellow brick sidewalk.

"Oh, no!" Howie yelled. "We forgot about Eddie. He's still in there! What if Miss Brewbaker finds him snooping in the kitchen?" The four kids looked back at the house. From inside they heard an eerie cackling. Then all was silent.

"What if Miss Brewbaker turned him into a frog?" Melody said.

Carey laughed. "What are you talking

about? Eddie isn't a frog, even though he might be a little slimy sometimes!"

"Very funny, bunny brains," Eddie said from behind them.

"Eddie, you're all right!" Melody threw her arms around him and gave him a big hug.

"Let go of me," Eddie snapped. He pushed her away and took a big bite from a huge red apple. "Of course, I'm all right. I *told* you I was too tough for a witch."

"What happened?" Howie asked.

Eddie spoke softly. "I found the cookbook, or rhyme book, or spell book, or whatever you want to call it. Then I said each one backwards, just like Howie said in his plan. I bet it broke every one of Miss Brewbaker's spells."

"I think you're right," Melody laughed as Prince Diamond came loping up and licked her right on the nose.

"Diamond!" Eddie yelled and hugged the big dog around the neck. "I'm so glad to see you!" Just then Merlin darted out from under a bush. Diamond gave a quick yelp, and raced down the street after the black cat.

"No!" Liza screamed. But she was too late.

12

Sleeping Beauty

"Where's Eddie?" Liza whispered the next day.

"He's going to miss the whole thing if he doesn't get here soon," Melody said softly. Miss Brewbaker's students were waiting to perform their flips for their parents.

Howie looked at his parents in the audience and waved. Next to Howie's mom sat Mr. Cooper with Snookems. "Maybe Prince Diamond ran away again," Howie said.

"I thought we'd never find him yesterday," Liza said.

"That dog is going to drive us crazy," Melody muttered. "He's always running off."

"Speaking of driving us crazy," Carey said. "There's Eddie now." The four kids watched as Eddie's grandmother dragged him through the door of the gym. Eddie yawned and walked over to line up with the other gymnasts.

"He looks like Sleeping Beauty," Liza giggled.

Carey shook her head. "There's nothing beautiful about Eddie." The kids had to agree that Eddie had never looked worse. His hair was mussed, his ball cap was on sideways, and he had dark circles under his eyes. He yawned again on his way over to them and nearly tripped on his untied shoelace.

"Oh, no!" Melody suddenly remembered. "Eddie ate that apple yesterday. Maybe Miss Brewbaker really did have a magic spell on it! He looks like he can't wake up."

"I didn't eat a rotten apple," Eddie

snapped. "I let Prince Diamond sleep in my room so he wouldn't run away again. He kept me up half the night, licking me in the face!"

"You mean he kissed you?" Howie asked.

Eddie rolled his eyes. "I wouldn't exactly call dog slobber a kiss."

Melody jumped up and down. "Diamond saved your life! If he hadn't kissed you last night you'd be in dreamland after eating Miss Brewbaker's magic apple."

"That's right." Howie nodded. "A kiss from a prince is the only thing that can save you from a witch's poison apple. Prince Diamond saved you."

"What's all this stuff about magic and witches?" Carey asked.

Liza shook her head. "These guys think Miss Brewbaker is a witch and her rhymes are magic spells."

Carey rolled her eyes. "That's the craziest thing I've ever heard," she said, looking at the yawning Eddie. "After all, witches don't do backflips."

Debbie Dadey and Marcia Thornton Jones have fun writing stories together. When they both worked at an elementary school in Lexington, Kentucky, Debbie was the school librarian and Marcia was a teacher. During their lunch break in the school cafeteria, they came up with the idea of the Bailey School kids.

Recently Debbie and her family moved to Plano, Texas. Marcia and her husband still live in Kentucky where she continues to teach. How do these authors still write together? They talk on the phone and use computers and fax machines!